Tudor
Mojeul

2017

"...human life, seen through human eyes, sometimes fortunate, sometimes unfortunate, neither perfect nor imperfect; it simply was, and is..."

RH Cunningham, 1911 - 2006

Life
Dances

Incorporating the six winning stories from the
RH Cunningham Memorial Short Story
Competition, 2017

For

Robert and Christine

Copyright Notice

LIFE DANCES © Willowdown Books 2017

1
Life Dances
Maynard, Trevor (Ed.)
Willowdown Books
ISBN-13: 978-1548631246
ISBN-10: 1548631248

Acknowledgements:

To all the authors who have so kindly contributed their work, and especially to my uncle, Robert Frederick Cunningham, for allowing me to use his book THE CUNNINGHAMS as a source material for my own story, "The Dance" based on the journals of my grandfather, in whose honour this book is created. To my wife Jo, who tirelessly gave her skills as editor, proof-reader, and sounding board: my darling, your patience may often have been frayed, but we are still here, and I love you. To my Mum, who encouraged me in producing the book, and who kindly agreed to read the final six stories. Finally, to the editorial team for their difficult task of selecting the winning entry.

Cover design, Trevor Maynard, photograph of RH Cunningham, aged 29, origin unknown. Back cover photographs © the authors.

Life Dances

Edited by Trevor Maynard

2017

CONTENTS

Introduction

How this anthology came into being...

Since 2010, I have run and edited a poetry anthology series called *THE POETIC BOND*, and in 2016, the first ideas of a complementary competition for short stories emerged. However, what form it would take, was still unclear.

To gauge interest, I set a snap flash fiction contest, and sought entries from professional writing forums on LinkedIN. From the response, it was clear there was a space for a more substantial contest, with the publishing of a paperback anthology as the goal; however, it was not until I began reading my grandfather's handwritten journals, that the theme, and indeed the purpose, of such an anthology became clear. The anthology would be both a tribute to my grandfather, and a platform for exciting new writing.

The Competition Brief

Willowdown Books invited submissions to a competition named in honour of RH Cunningham, for a short story between 1,000 and 2,000 words, written in English, with a reward of publication for six stories, and a prize of $100 for the top story. The theme was as follows:

"The prize is in honour of RH Cunningham, the grandfather of the editor, who served in the Royal Navy during World War Two; he later joined the Merchant Navy and served as Chief Steward. He travelled the world, and so the object of each story should be to open the reader's eyes to the wider world we live in, or, shed an interesting perspective on past or present events, or reflect on personal and social journeys; in essence, to look at the world anew. This can mean the theme is travel, or nature, or society, but is not restricted to these."

The competition opened for submissions on January 1st, 2017, and closed on March 31st, 2017. Winners were notified on 30th June, and the publication date from this volume of July 31st, 2017

I am very pleased, and honoured, many people sent in their stories, and it was a great pleasure to read such an eclectic and fascinating selection. Six have been chosen for publication, and one, for the first prize of $100.

For me, it seemed only fitting that the voice of RH Cunningham himself be heard in this collection. He was, after all, a bit of a raconteur, with many colourful stories to tell, and who had led a long and fascinating life. He was certainly never shy of giving advice, was a generous host to strangers and friends alike, and of course, an elegant and consummate ballroom dancer.

From my grandfather's many handwritten journals, I adapted a short story *The Dance*. To complete this journey, I have also included a short story from my own grand-daughter. The resulting book, through the imaginations of an eclectic and entertaining collection of writers, I hope, will help you, the reader, to view the world anew.

Trevor Maynard, July 2017

No Going Back

SANDY NORRIS

Mid-morning but already the day is warm - almost hot. The ship drifts along the coast of Montenegro - sails drooping - engines hardly audible. The mountains are serene, the sky is blue and around me plenty of passengers lie comatose on their loungers.

Perfection.

But my reality is quite different. While I stand on the quarter deck outwardly calm, panic is rising up the backs of my legs - up through my stomach - to my shoulders – to my throat. I swallow but choke. I look up and see the two feet of a girl gone before me as she completes her climb; pulls herself up the last stretch of rope and disappears through the hole up into the crow's nest. She makes it look so easy – as though she might do it every day of her life. Only it won't be like that. She's just brave.

And now the next one is half-way up it's my turn. My attempt to climb the ship's mast. I'm scared I'm going to wet myself. Wonder briefly, whether I'm more frightened of failing or of falling.

Wearing sensible pumps and longish shorts, feet pasted to the deck, I balance while Don, the activity organiser, helps me into the harness. One at a time my legs go through wide buckled leather straps. They link to another strap around my waist and everything is yanked tight. So tight I feel I can't breathe. But that's ridiculous - the top part of my body is free. I try to visualise what would happen if I slipped and they weren't holding the rope properly... I know I wouldn't crash down onto the deck - but would I swing folded down in half to make the weight of a pendulum?

I imagine my body strung up in the air like a turkey hung in a butcher's shop, waiting for Christmas...

People I know at work write me off because I'm shy. I'm the one who never has a boyfriend. They sneer when they think I'm not looking. I know they do, although they wouldn't admit it. They're too polite. I don't do online dating. I wouldn't trust it. At office parties I get through by standing near someone, trying to look content, hoping they will want to talk to me, because I can never find anything interesting to say to them. I booked onto this cruise to try and make friends. There are only two hundred passengers and I'm hoping I might do better with the smaller group.

Last year I tried one of the big ships, but that was a disaster. With two thousand people milling around, I just felt lonely the whole time. Everyone was in a family group – or a group of friends - or as one of a couple...

Don nods to show it's time and clinging to the shrouds, I small-step right along the edge of the deck to where he points, aware that its only half a step backwards to topple over the edge of the ship and into the sea below. A beautiful blue-green August sea reflecting its colour off the mountains – but deep, so very deep. My mind takes me under the surface, drops me lower and lower where the water will be cold, makes me watch as the hull of the ship slips past and leaves me...

I watch him as he twists the safety clip of my harness, see his strong brown fingers working the metal, hear it click shut onto his rope. I tilt my head backwards, feeling inadequate – look up and observe the fore mast standing silent. Waiting.

See not only the cloudless blue sky but also my imminent destination: a tiny square hole probably thirty metres above the deck in the underside of the look-out platform.

The climber before me is nearly up.

For another minute I stand and wait while Don pulls at the red-flecked safety rope to check it's in place. 'Okay?' he says. So I nod – no longer having any choice - and reach out with my right hand to take hold of the metal stay. Then I lift my left foot and place it carefully on the first rung; but with a shock I feel the sway - the lack of firmness in the foothold. I've never climbed a rope ladder before – only a firm metal one at home to go up into the loft. I grip the rope so tightly it burns into my palms, haul myself up with muscles that are over-tense, fumble to place my right foot alongside my left. But that now shifts the rope in the opposite direction. The stretch between rungs is quite big – thirty or forty centimetres and I realise I'm shivering.

Keep breathing.

Keep moving

Don't look down

Keep moving

Don't look down.

But I do.

I see by the positioning of people's heads below me on either side, that I am already about the height of a man above the deck. And at a frightening angle. But what did I expect? The shrouds have to angle in. Of course they do. They're responsible for holding the mast in place.

Out of sight now, Don will be holding the rope that goes all the way up to the lookout platform and back down to my harness. And I have to believe in him. The crowd of watchers grows and through my fear I do sense a whisper of pride that I am doing this while they are not. I risk another look. Realise the crowd has become thirty or forty.

After about ten upward steps my foot fumbles, missing the rope and there is a collective gasp from below. I force a grin. A fixed grin which conceals fear. Know I need to pretend that I am loving every minute.

While I climb I think again of the first girl who was so quick. Everyone will compare our different speeds. But too bad. I make a rhythm in my head and chant it silently to keep me moving:

Right hand up.

Lift left foot.

Left hand up.

Lift right foot.

DON'T LOOK DOWN.

Right hand up.

Lift left foot.

Left hand up.

Lift right foot.

And after an interval, the next climber starts up after me. The rope quivers in my hands as he sets a rhythm adrift of mine. I climb higher. Leave the shadow of the sails below. Feel the burn of the sun through my cotton tee-shirt and the stream of sweat running down between my breasts. The side seam of my shorts has caught in the harness and chafes against my inner thighs.

But I am making progress.

The last stage - which I thought would be better, given that I am nearly at the end – suddenly opens up to view. The vertical shrouds now mesh with a stretch of ropes on a slant, angling across and as I creep upwards I find I need to transfer from one to the other, to position myself under the hole.

Stop.

Can't think how to move.

Until I hear a voice from above: 'Reach across with your right hand to the extreme edge of the cross rope... That's right... now shift your right foot...

And I rotate and lever my body up – back into the sun. I sit on the floor of the lookout next to the feet of the girl in charge, trying to slow my breathing, while she leans down to unclip the rope and send it back to Don. When I pull myself up behind the safety of the canvas wall of the platform, I feel the breeze in my face and within seconds, I'm drying out. I peer over the side and find I'm smiling.

Ahead and below, the bows of the clipper sweep cleanly through the water. Astern, are the other masts, their rigging in a row behind mine. Underneath, I see the queue of other people waiting to do what I have just done...

In the evening I change into a dress and head for the bar on the main deck. Surely now I can talk to someone. I have something to say. I take a large glass of wine from the tray being carried round. Look for any familiar face. And over on the side, see a quiet guy called Simon who sometimes sits on the same table at dinner. I slip through between the larger groups and stand quite close, looking anywhere but at him. I pretend to be absorbed in the music played by the local band who have come on board when we anchored. Wait for the right moment to turn and say something.

But he beats me to it.

'Do you mind if I join you?' he says. Then he smiles.

'You were one of the first up the mast today, weren't you? You looked as though you were really enjoying yourself.'

I drink about half my glassful in one go. Feel the effect swilling through me.

'Actually, I was quite scared.'

'So why did you do it then?'

'Oh – you know – bit of a challenge.'
'Hey that's cool. I wouldn't do it, I'm not brave enough – I mean I've wanted to talk to you all week, but I haven't dared.'

Suspicious, I study his face; thinking he must be mocking me. But from his expression I realise he's not joking. In fact he looks embarrassed.

'Why not?' A bit blunt, but my brain has closed down.

'I'm just me.'

He shakes his head. Swigs some more wine and puts his glass down on a table. 'I can never tell what you're thinking. Honest. None of us can.' I stare at this stranger, stunned that they've even bothered to discuss me. I notice a tic in his neck, as though he's nervous, and I can't think of any response at all, so I wait for him to carry on.

"Look I'm not trying to be rude, but you're so quiet, it almost seems like you don't want to join in.'

'That's rubbish,' I blush. Shocked.

The band swinging into a noisy rumba wraps us closer together in an uneasy silence. I could easily reach out for his hand, only I don't have the nerve.

'The other guys on the table think you're too clever for them.'

'But I'm not...'

He shrugs. 'They don't know that, because you never say anything.' He grabs his glass again and I see he's sweating. Am I so frightening? They don't know me at all. I finish my drink and pick up another as the waiter drifts past. Simon does the same.

'I really like you, you seem just my type, but – well I s'pose I've messed up now.' He looks down at the deck and keeps talking, but the noise from the band is so loud that I have to step right up to him to hear. 'I know we aren't supposed to have gender roles these days, but as a bloke I'm still feeling I ought to make the first move' – his words tumble out in a rush. 'You're not the only one who's shy, you know.' He looks up, smiles sadly and turns away, leaving me on my own.

I stand dumb for several seconds, taking it in. And now my heart starts thumping. Anticipating. I move after him. Walk faster, needing to catch up. Cross my fingers, hoping I'm getting this right. Reach out and touch his shoulder. As he swings round, I look straight at him and smile. 'There's another mast climbing slot tomorrow. Why don't you have a go and I'll come and watch?'

TOO MUCH

Israela Margalit

At the red light she said that he was a loser and she had no idea why she'd married him, as she had many times before.

As the traffic light turned green he veered to the right and said he was sorry she felt that way, as he had many times before.

They stopped at the "Jody's Mirage" gas station for her bathroom break, as they had many times before.

She walked to the bathroom with gusto and closed the door behind her. He drove to the makeshift parking lot in the back. He lit a cigarette, sucked in the nicotine that savored his body like no woman had done for a long time, and exhaled the fumes in a fog wave that shielded him momentarily from the dim light of his dismal existence. Those were the motions of his life, day in and day out, as repetitive and predictable as shovels clearing snow in winter.

But then he couldn't take it one minute longer. He put the cigarette down, pressed on the gas and took off toward the highway.

It was not as spontaneously reckless an act as it might seem. He had been daydreaming about how he'd watch her walk to the bathroom door, how he'd park in the back, how he'd light a cigarette, and how he'd be overcome by a surge of courage that would propel him to push on the gas, drive to the highway, and disappear from her life as if sucked into a sinkhole; but, while he basked in the joy of his illusory self, his right foot always lifted itself off the brake pedal and slid onto the accelerator, compelling his hands to guide the slow crawl back to the gas station just as she stepped out of the bathroom ready to climb into the passenger seat. Defeated by a limb, he dutifully drove her back home, ate her expertly cooked dinner, washed the dirty dishes, and staggered from another dreary evening into the blissful oblivion of a night sleep.

But today—today something happened to his foot. Must have been the new sneakers. His cheeks flushed red, his pulse quickened. Was this how it felt to be a man?

A distant police siren reminded him to be cautious. Steady on the gas. If he drove carefully, he could vanish. He had time. She used to take at least fifteen minutes in the bathroom, no matter how many people with bursting bladders were knocking on the door. That was one cause of their interminable fights, but now it was a source of comfort because it gave him a precious fifteen-minute head start on the rest of his life.

He drove on the country road leading to the highway and pondered his route. He could go to New London some fifty miles north, check into a bed-and-breakfast under a false name, then take the ferry. The thought of being at a bed-and-breakfast all by himself lifted his spirits. He'd take off his clothes and throw them on the floor. He'd sing at the top of his lungs in the shower with the bathroom door wide open. Then he'd sleep late, have a lazy breakfast, and pour extra syrup on his pancakes.

She wouldn't find him. Even if she could find him, she wouldn't. He knew exactly what she'd do. She'd come out of the bathroom and wait for him to pick her up. She always expected him to pick her up at the exact moment she stepped out of the bathroom, and when he was late, she gave him the silent treatment. That was another cause for their interminable fights.

The traffic on the country road came to a halt as he neared the railroad crossing. He lit a cigarette and waited. She would be out of the bathroom by now. In ten minutes she'd begin to wonder where he was. She'd reluctantly walk to the parking space in the back, her disapproval of him at a boiling point. She'd look around casually for the car, but when she didn't find it, she'd shed some of her smugness. She'd ask around if anybody had seen an indistinct driver in an indistinct car, and they'd say yes, they had, there were many of those.

He could hear the approaching sound of the engine and the turning of wheels on the railroad track. In a few minutes the train will have passed and he'd be heading to the exit that would take him to the highway. By that time she'd have realized that he was no longer in the vicinity of the gas station. She'd swallow her pride and call his cell. There would be no answer. She'd text "Your ringer is off. Call me." The absence of a reply would baffle her. She'd call Jody's brother, then Jody himself, but no one would have any information about his whereabouts. Jody would ask if they'd had a fight. She'd say they had, but they always had fights so that was nothing of significance. Jody would say that sometimes an extra push could be a game changer, and maybe she had overdone it. She would counter that Jody didn't understand the dynamics of her marriage. He'd never take off without letting her know and gaining her approval. That was why she was going to call 911, just in case he had gotten into some kind of trouble. The police would tell her that there had been no accident involving the car in question, and she couldn't file a missing person report for at least twenty-four hours, because if they'd searched for every husband who'd gone out to run an errand and didn't show up for dinner, they'd have no time to stop bank robberies and terrorist attacks. That would be when it dawned on her that he might have left her, as unlikely as such a scenario might seem. "Let the moron go, who needs him," would be her likely reaction while climbing into bed to watch her soaps on TiVo, which was another cause of their interminable fights.

He could hear the train whistle as it forged ahead away from the crossing, the wheels grinding as it gained speed. Traffic was about to start moving again. He put down his cigarette and reached for another, then changed his mind. His pack was half empty. As soon as he gained safe distance he would buy a carton with his credit card. Their credit card. By tomorrow she'll have canceled it. She'd say it was stolen and get a new one, the numbers of which he wouldn't be privy to. But wait a moment. The credit card company would inform her that the last transaction was for a carton of Marlboros, and that would tell her everything she needed to know: that he was alive, that he was in control of his actions, that he was not all that far away—his entire plan was in jeopardy. A crisis was looming. He couldn't use his credit card, and he was short on cash. He definitely didn't have enough for a night at a B&B as well as a carton of cigarettes. Their ATM card was in her handbag. He carried on him the family credit card, and she their ATM card. That was one of the few things they agreed on, measures to protect themselves from theft or loss of personal documents. He knew he wouldn't be able to go through with his flight without nicotine. Of that he was certain. A man about to relinquish everything needed a crutch. He should turn around and go home, retrieve a few cartons from his hidden stash in the garage, and rush back to the highway. She wouldn't be back yet. She had no car with her. By the time she called Jody's brother, called Jody, called the police and then found someone to drive her back home, he'd get to the garage and back.

The left lane was empty as the train barriers began to lift. He swerved the car a hundred and eighty degrees, and speeded home. The swift move filled him with confidence. He had never been a daring driver, and now he'd maneuvered the car with the intrepid hands of a pro.

All was quiet when he got to the house, the lone security light flickering on and off as it had for a while. Maybe he should change the bulb, so she'd know that he had the temerity to go to the house before the big escape. That would give her pause after years of branding him a coward. It galvanized him that she was not there, that his calculations had been correct. When was the last time he was right about anything? He opened the large box at the back of the garage, removed the riffraff on the top, reached down for his cartons— all three of them—and transferred them to his trunk. His bladder demanded attention. He hurried to the tiny toilet by the kitchen and relieved himself.

On the way back he passed by the hall closet, and grabbed his coat. It would be a good idea to go to the bedroom in the back and fetch some clothing items plus his laptop. He was cognizant of time passing and the danger of her imminent return, but —electrified by his new self-awareness—he relished the suspense. That was the new him. Someone who took a risk and prevailed.

His arms loaded with clothing items, the computer bag on his shoulder, he crossed through the kitchen to the garage door for the last time. Something smelled good. What day was it? Thursday? Thursday was lamb stew night. He looked at the slow cooker. The red light was on. Stew done. Keeping warm.

"Hungry?"

He was not startled by the voice. He had taken a chance coming to the house and then procrastinating. He turned around.

He looked at Jody. "What are you doing here?"

"Waiting for you. I thought you'd come back at some point."

"Did she send you?"

"She was livid when she couldn't find you. I suggested that she stay at the station until I got some news."

"She's used to being in control.'

"No longer. You've made your point."

"I haven't even started."

"I think she's got it."

"They say that people are affected by trauma for six months, then its memory fades away. How long do you think she'll remember my five-minute act of disobedience?"

Jody sniffed the stew.
"She a good cook?"

"What's the difference? She puts me down at dinner and the food gets stuck in my throat."

"Can I have a taste? I'm starving."

"She won't like it, you eating her food before she says it's time."

"You paid for the food. You can decide."
He stopped dead in his tracks. Jody was right. He paid his share. This was his stew as much as it was hers.

Jody watched him carefully. "Come on, man. We can talk while we eat."

"And if she comes back before we finish?"

"What are you afraid of? You've done nothing wrong."

Jody was right again. There was no reason for him to run away like a thief in the night. He deserved a good meal before embarking on his long trip. Jody retrieved two bowls from the cupboard, filled one, then another. He put them on the table.

"Where are the spoons?"

"In the drawer over there," he said.

The stew emitted a heat-induced light haze. His stomach was rumbling. There was a warm meal on the table and the spoons were in the drawer. That was his life. He had done nothing wrong. Apart from squashing her dreams, squandering her love, and extinguishing the light in her eyes, he had done nothing wrong. But what about his dreams? His passions? Hadn't she wiped out his memory of who he used to be?

He stood by the door. Jody looked at him.

"Coming?"

When
Food
Kills

Belinda DuPret

It was odd, but visiting day wasn't embarrassing. I'd expected an icy reception, or at least a very cold shoulder, but he gave a cheery smile and kissed my cheek. Very charitable when you consider the things I'd said in court a few weeks ago - all pounced on by the media which, as a result painted him as a freakish and deadly eating machine. He'd lost weight since then – at least forty pounds - and looked a hell of a lot better.

Lucy, his wife, would have been pleased, because his ever-increasing girth was a continuous bone of contention between them, and he was bound to lose even more body-fat over the next 12 years – or whatever.

Chris Sinclair was an old University friend. We'd met in the early 1970s, rather fancied each other for a while and even talked briefly of marriage then drifted apart. He'd moved steadily upwards in the banking world whilst I, also very good with numbers - but in a different kind of way, became a magician for a while, then gave that up for professional gambling and moved from London to Las Vegas where competitions abounded.

Playing games of chance became my passion with Poker at the top of the list, while he loved Lucy, a young, lithe and Garbo-esque champion skier – and Toilet Tissue heiress. Their marriage attracted headlines here and there, mainly along the lines of "London Banker marries Paper Money!"

Since then I'd heard nothing, until last year, when I won a major international poker competition and ended up on some predictable TV Chat shows which led to a rash of invitations from PR Companies I'd never heard of, and some nearly-forgotten old acquaintances, most of which I turned down. However, a "Divorced and Delighted" party did tickle my sense of humour and that was where I spotted Chris, spearing an escargot with a platinum toothpick. I know it was platinum because he proudly told me so, adding that it was a recent gift from a special person.

Twelve years had added at least three hundred pounds to his frame – he was nearly thrice the man he used to be. In fact, he was more than paunchy, corpulent, or even extremely fat. He was morbidly obese, but still recognisable as the man I'd nearly married. I congratulated him on the marriage he had made, silently grateful he'd wed the toilet-paper heiress instead of me, and asked if Lucy was at the party.

"Oh" he said, with a sigh. "Lucy. Now that was a big mistake!" Then delicately, with the tip of his tongue he caught some Muscat-flavoured sauce dripping off a sliver of charcoal-seared octopus, he'd just "tooth-picked", then sensuously wrapped his tongue round it, pulled it voluptuously into his mouth and swallowed –

like a fleshy lizard savouring a nice fat blowfly. The morsel ingested he settled with a satisfied sigh into the deeply padded sofa.

As Chris had been the most easy-going man in the world, I was surprised his marriage hadn't worked, and said so.

"Did you ever meet Lucy?" he asked, morosely. I shook my head and grabbed a bottle of vintage Gruard Larose from a passing tray. Chris looked like someone about to open the floodgates of self-pity so I knocked back a fast glass for sustenance, poured another and settled back to listen.

"Lucy was gorgeous when I met her" he began. "Beautiful, stylish clever – everything a chap could ever dream of...." He stopped talking and sat shaking his head as if totally bewildered. "Mmmmhhmmm?" I said encouragingly, and waited for the more I knew was certainly coming.

Chris filled his glass with a Batard-Montrachet that, (according to a waiter) had breathed for the required time (oh yes, it was that kind of party!) and swirled it gently to release the bouquet, then sipped and rolled it thoughtfully round his palate before finally swallowing. It was obvious this was going to take time, so I slipped a deck of cards from my handbag and quietly shuffled. It always whiled away boring moments and kept my hands supple – not necessary for a poker player, but I enjoyed the dexterity. Plus a few card tricks always made people smile. As I deftly palmed four aces he shook his head gently and started to talk, genuine sadness echoing in his voice.

"I really miss Lucy. Honest Nicky, she was special. Sparkling, eager, passionate - and into everything! Scuba-diving, dancing, ski-ing. And her mouth was so voluptuous!" He sighed, ate more octopus then continued. "She was really beautiful! Honestly, she glowed!" He sighed heavily in emphasis then continued. "It was her joie de vivre – I loved. She had real joie de vivre. It made me feel happy and alive just to be with her. Well, it did in the beginning."

He paused to flag down a passing trolley of chargrilled sanglier which was artistically topped with a fattening dollop of bone-marrow persillade, heaped his plate high and proceeded to seriously eat, not noticing the oil and sauce dripping down his chin in greasy little rivulets, and falling onto his clothes.

My playing cards rippled from hand to hand, making a fountain, then two fountains, (all bloody clever stuff) but he never noticed, not even when I made one card pop up and wriggle at him.

To be honest, I was getting bored. Deeply, stultifyingly bored. After all, there was an obvious ending to all this - she'd got fed up with his obsessive eating, and his ever- increasing size, and left him.

Eventually he stopped eating long enough to catch his breath and went on with his story. "A man can have too much of a good thing" he pronounced suddenly, then continued eating with ferocious intensity.

Nothing can break that kind of concentration, so I flicked a card at the ceiling where it stuck, just as it was meant to do, then waved to the newly-divorced (and presumably delighted) hostess: a creamy, full fat, matte grosse (with only a few blue veins) forty-two year old called Felicity. "Lovely party!" I carolled to her fat round bottom, which was all I could see. "Wonderful food!" She was pressing bocconcini topped with spiced lentils and choritzo onto another guest, so didn't reply, just signified she'd heard with a flap of her prettily dimpled podgy hand.

Felicity had made all the food herself, as she'd emphasized when I arrived. "I love food!" she said. "This lot..." (a wave indicating tables piled with food) "It took hours in the kitchen but oh, so so worth it" and Chris obviously agreed – he blew a languid kiss in her direction, heaved a balsamic-scented sigh in mine and went on with his story.

"It was wonderful at first" he confided "But Lucy turned out to be a vampire! A vitality vampire! She sucked out my energy and lived off it. She jogged every morning and tap-danced at night. Even at weekends, and I was TOTALLY

shagged!" He flopped his head forward in demonstration and almost absent-mindedly ate a comforting platter of Barolo-basted woodchuck then slumped sideways, seemingly stupefied by food.

" Climb this, ski there, bobsleigh that!" he suddenly burst out, making me muff a complex one-handed dealers-shuffle. He drew a deep sobbing breath, with his face showing indignation and self-pity then he drew another deep sobbing breath before continuing bravely "But I coped. I slept in while she jogged and I had breakfast while she ski'd. And most afternoons she explored galleries or ruins while I had a nap and a snack. Then she did Pilates while I found somewhere decent for dinner – it can be jolly hard finding a good restaurant every night, you know" he said, almost accusingly, then subsided.

I thought he'd eaten himself into a food-induced coma, but he roused and started talking again. "We were rubbing along nicely considering how tired I was, which was all her fault. But then, out of the blue, Lucy said I was overweight!" The memory obviously hurt, because his face crumpled, like a child's does when it's about to cry; his chin was a moon-surface of dimples, and he burrowed his abundant backside even deeper into the cushions – before leaning forward to sample some Moroccan chicken with preserved lemons proffered by an attentive waiter. Food can be a real comfort, especially when dealing with obviously distressing memories.

"Lucy banned cream and alcohol, and made me go to the gym!   Then she gave away all my tins of pâté de foie gras and duck confit. Removing temptation, she called it".

He gave a rather fat-rippling shudder of remembered angst, tossed back an Armagnac (for the digestion presumably) and continued his tale of woe.

"I lost weight and toned up, but she still wasn't happy. She wanted us to DO things together. To DO things! Outdoorsy, energetic things!" A frisson of horror ran through his frame at the memory, and he was so distressed he didn't even notice that I'd turned a ten into a King with just a tap of a finger.

Felicity arrived just then, in an aromatic swirl of garlic, cinnamon, lumache and lace and Chris recovered enough sang-froid to sample her hot pastrami, smiling thanks through mouthfuls of food.

"I'm sorry it didn't work" I said, silently doffing an invisible hat to the absent Lucy. What a

girl! How on earth had she stomached this gargantuan eating machine for even a short amount of time?

"Well, you know me" he said. "Silly Arse. I'll do anything to keep the peace". He shifted his bulk

to a more comfortable position and went on. "We walked, swam, sky-dived, and even pot-holed together, but climbing glaciers was tooooo much. It was always freezing and wet, so I severed the matrimonial cord. Lucy was furious! I can still hear her screaming abuse at me".

"She was angry?" I asked, surprised. I thought she'd have been delighted!

"Livid" he said, making a naughty, fat-boy face. "But that's life" and he heaped two plates high with blinis, soured cream and black caviar and handed me one. "See!" he said smiling. "I remember you like Russian food".
It was almost like old times as we ate together, and afterwards, as he spooned massive portions of chocolate galette (with a warm sauce of caramel chunks and crushed cashews) into his mouth, he confided that he wasn't soured by the matrimonial disaster with Lucy in any way at all. No, not at all. He'd recently met his ideal

woman, proposed to Felicity and was very keen to jump into her matrimonial hot-pot.

"But only" he whispered, leaning forward, and tapping the side of his nose.... "Only when they recover poor Lucy's body from that Norwegian glacier. I want to feel, well, totally safe, if you get my drift!"

I dropped my cards through paralysed fingers as I realised – he hadn't just severed the matrimonial cord, he'd cut the safety rope and killed the poor bitch.

True North

Lynne Zotalis

My long-time friend, Suzan, and I date back to the early 70's, where we met on a mountain range, Mesa Poleo, in the Santa Fe National Forest. Past the Abiqui Dam, where Georgia O'Keefe lived, in Northern New Mexico, hippies found a bit of Shangri La, building log cabins intending to live out our days away from society's ills. Thirty-five plus years later, we remain close friends, even though my permanent residence is 1400 miles north in Decorah, Iowa. We've outlived our husbands; hers, Mark, dropped dead of a heart attack a year and a half ago; mine, Chuck, was asphyxiated seven years ago when he aspirated salt water, snorkelling in Tulum, Mexico, where we were celebrating our 30th wedding anniversary.

My devastation and shock were so debilitating, so pervasive, that I could barely function for two years. My four adult children truly wondered if I'd survive. I am forever altered, enormously challenged, and able to see beyond the pain now, all these years later. Suzan and I both contend that getting outside, breathing in the fresh air, and clearing the cobwebs have been integral in aiding the grief process.

On the arduous journey to recovery, we have shared strength, encouraging each other to keep on, to never, never, never give in, and to remember that we still are, in our hearts, mountain women. When Suzan asked if I wanted to join her for an extreme Alaskan adventure, I immediately jumped onboard. So last May, we pushed body, mind, and spirit to the limit signing up for the most outrageous side trips offered on a 10-day excursion, beginning in Anchorage and ending in Vancouver.

Not only were we transported to another state – one that hardly felt like part of the U.S. – but it seemed as though we'd been relocated to another world. And on each leg of our journey by land, air, and sea, we moved farther from our comfort zone and a little closer to the edge.

A single engine, five-seater plane was our first mode of transport. It took us above the Talkeetna glacier. Talkeetna was the strange little village quite accurately depicted in the early 90's T.V. series, Northern Exposure. We were supposed to be able to set down and walk about, but the weather was snowy with low visibility. Our veteran pilot wisely opted to forego the dangerous landing.

Exchanging air for rails in the pursuant train ride to Denali, glimpsing the singular beauty throughout the isolated countryside, we were very fortunate to see Mt. McKinley 'come out' on a couple of occasions. At twenty thousand feet it possesses its own weather system, so many travellers wait for days to see it only to be disappointed.

The next leg of our journey was an exhilarating white-water raft trip down the Nenana River including one category four rapid and several threes. The 32.5F-degree water left me breathless as icy waves blasted my face. Definitely an adrenaline rush! The guide explained that the water was a mere four hours from the glacier. "Are we going to be able to do this?" I questioned Suzan, after an attempt to thaw out my bones in a steaming shower.

"Either that or we'll die trying," she joked.

Almost every morning we travelled to a new destination. Fairbanks was low-key with a steamboat ride to an Athabaskan Village where we learned the native lore from two young women back from college for the summer. The Athabaskans, late prehistoric and historic period peoples of the American southwest, are considered ancestral to the Navajo and Apache.

Athabaskan tribes originated in Canada and the Northern Territories migrating into the American southwest sometime after 1400 AD. Suzan, having lived and worked in the Southwest, was able to converse in Navajo, albeit primitively, with a ninety-six-year-old Athabaskan man that we encountered. Home to Iditarod mushers, one of the local sayings is: "Fairbanks—where men are strong and women win the Iditarod." Another is: "If you're looking for a man, the odds are good, but the goods are odd." No argument there. About five men to one woman. This was pre-Sarah Palin notoriety or we may have sat that one out.

Being two women, we kept a wary eye for ten men chasing us on to Juneau, Alaska's state capital. The fact that one can't reach the town via highway—you can only get there by plane or boat—was certainly telling. The residents like it that way and sport bumper stickers saying, "If you want more roads, move south." It truly seems like another planet and so did the experience of trekking around on the glacier. It is something akin to traveling backward through time a couple million years. Mendenhall Glacier field, North America's fifth largest ice field, is located in the Coast Mountain Range and blankets fifteen hundred square miles of land. The vastness is incomprehensible. Trying to put the size of the Mendenhall Glacier field into perspective from the front seat of the helicopter was dizzying. After landing, we donned the provided gear, much of which, although likely to help us, could also injure us if used improperly. Crampons are spiked add-ons that you strap to the bottom of your boots, enabling you to keep a steady foothold on ice, but if you trip you can easily slice a leg with the metal points. Gloves, we were told, had to be worn at all times. The guide warned us about the hazards posed to our palms sliding across the ice surface that resembled shards of broken glass. The ice-pick walking stick helped us stay upright on the slippery hike, but without the proper caution could impale someone if landed upon. A helmet topped off the 'protective' outfit.

Each and every guide had an impressive knowledge, ability, and genuine love of Alaska. Not many of them live there year-round, but returned for the season to infuse tourists with wanderlust. I positioned myself directly behind the lead guide, placing my foot in his imprint. To my untrained eye it was all solid, but you could easily break through softer spots and end up in a crevasse with one misstep. The astounding blue/white peaks glistened as the sun streamed across, virtually blinding us if we took our sunglasses off. The two miles went by much too quickly.

But despite my enjoyment of our glacial trek, I must admit my favorite adventure was the sheer rock climb in Skagway, coupled with rappelling back down. Each challenge was carefully prefaced with instructions and proper gear. I always felt secure with the tools afforded us. The intense physical exertion along with the technical difficulty taxed me to my limit.

Being harnessed was reassuring but as the 40F degree weather turned my fingertips numb, I determined that faith and fortitude would have to guide my assent. More than once I thought, "This is so nuts, am I crazy?" Reaching the top, one, two, and finally, the third and highest climb, it gave me such a sense of accomplishment that it was well worth the trepidation. I would absolutely do it again.

Suzan and I loved the looks we got from those younger and more experienced than us, but evident also, were the encouraging words, that spurred us on.

"You can do this. Hang on! Go for it!"

We were determined women that day, our age and experience propelling us toward our goal and ultimately the end of our Alaskan adventure.

We completed our journey high above the treetops in Ketchikan with a zip line that claimed to be the longest and fastest of its caliber in North America. The longest being eight hundred fifty feet, the highest, one hundred thirty five feet, and the fastest, thirty five miles per hour. The platform swayed as each member landed, which meant the tree that it was built upon was alive and healthy. Good to know. Three suspension bridges mixed it up a bit, giving us ample opportunity to observe the bears cavorting on the ground, dining on blueberries. Upon completion, we were all given medals, which I wore on the ship that night, proud to exhibit my prowess. We had done it, and we hadn't died trying. We really lived.

So I exhort all my fellow baby boomers, and really, anyone, to fulfill a dream this year. If you can muster the will, if you're fit and able, listen to your heart and follow that distant call. Hear your inner voice.

When Suzan asked me to go to Alaska, I was reminded of a conversation my husband and I had while trying to decide if we could splurge on Mexico. It was a milestone anniversary, we'd raised four children, two still completing college, and didn't really have the means to go on such an extravagant vacation.

I argued, "This is really a big deal. Thirty years is a rare gift. We have to do something special. What if we're not here next year?"

He wasn't.

The Death Of Rock 'n' Roll

Michael McLaughlin

Year 2067.

The radio station stood on Mexican soil on a desolate road in the center of the approaching Sonjave Desert. It was renamed when the Mojave and Sonora deserts merged into one large barren landscape and swallowed up parts of southwestern Arizona, and most of southern California to 100 miles south of Los Angeles. The desert sands even filled in the gulf of Cortez and one could walk across from Mazatlán to Cabo. The area was so barren and inhospitable that illegal American aliens coming down into Mexico did not dare walk into this death desert. But it was a perfect place for the last rock and roll radio station. Wolfman Jack broadcasted not too far from here a hundred years ago.

The small clapboard building was made of wood, a rare construction material. Blinking in one window was a red neon light with the letters KRZY RADIO. Behind the station, far out into the desert, forsaken buildings stood like half submerged reefs in a sea of brown sand and rock. Parked in front of the radio station was an old red hover craft fuelled by corn oil. The license plate read: RNR4EVER.

Inside the small studio the DJ stood behind the microphone and waved his arms around as he spoke. "Hello listeners, this is Emperor Norton coming at you from a clan....destine location. I'm the last man standing in this marathon of rock-n-roll music! And we're not going down without one last...." He hit a red button on the console and the sound effect of a big explosion boomed over the air. "As you may or may not know station KRZY..." He hit another button and a man babbled incoherently. "...is going off the air and with it rock-n-roll dies. So rockers, turn up your hearing aids, give yourself more oxygen, and listen to the greatest music of all time!" He hit another button and it was the sound of Muhammad Ali shouting, "The greatest of all time!"

"The next selection is a classic song by the poet laureate of rock-n-roll, Bobby Dylan."

...'Once upon a time you dressed so fine, threw the bums a dime in your prime, didn't you? People call say "beware doll, you're bound to fall" you thought they were all kidding you'...

The last DJ for rock-n-roll was Pepe Amadeus, or his radio name, Emperor Norton. He was a fourth generation DJ. His great grandfather played the first psychedelic music in San Francisco in the 1960's. Next to the control console was a faded picture of his great grandfather as a young man with shoulder-length hair, wire-rim glasses and a strange goatee. He wore bulky headphones, and with his long hair and sly smile, he looked like a demented praying mantis.

Emperor Norton was bald, a by-product of his generation's recreational use of dirty bombs in the United States around 2060. Atomic material was everywhere and any school boy could make a bomb.

Emperor Norton switched on the microphone. "So little time and so much music to play for the center of the universe called L.A." A needle dropped on a scratchy vinyl record. "Hey, that's right. I'm playing records, real records that haven't been heard in sixty years!"

As the music boomed over the speakers in the small studio, Emperor Norton took a crumpled marijuana joint from his shirt pocket. He still rolled his own instead of buying them in churches. With his flameless lighter he fired it up, inhaled deeply, and then let the smoke seep out his nose. He stared out the window at the barren desert and knew his music was dead. Nobody listened to rock-n-roll except for cliché songs like, The Monster Mash every Halloween. Even the standard, Dust in the Wind played at all funerals was heard less and less. Today's hip youth now listened to old Broadway show tunes from Guys and Dolls or The Sound of Music. My God, he hated that music.

The song was just about to end and he put the smoking joint on the edge of the console table. The edge was a neat row of black and brown burn marks.

"Grab your surf boards! Surf's up! This is by the Beach Boys around 1960 something. That's when we had a beach."

...'If everybody had an ocean, across the U.S.A, then everybody'd be surfin', like Californ-i-a. You'd see 'em wearing their baggies, huarache sandals too. A bushy, bushy blonde hairdo, surfin' U.S.A'...

He knew since the oceans had risen forty feet in the last forty years there weren't any waves. The scientific explanation was global warming had made the Pacific Ocean calmer. Plus, when the surf was up, it was too dangerous surfing between the buildings in the half-submerged cities of Long Beach, Malibu, and San Pedro.

With the joint burning in his mouth, the music blaring, he walked out to his parked hover craft and lugged in two cardboard boxes. Inside one box was his collection of rare vinyl records. Inside the other box was a remnant of his youth.

Emperor Norton sat down and worried what he was going to play for the very last song of rock-n-roll. The station had run a contest, but some far-out, nut spammer rigged the results and the song voted last one played was, *'Yummy, Yummy, Yummy, I Got Love in my Tummy.'* It was an obscure minor hit in the 1960s and, as the last guardian of the music, he would not go out with that sugary love snivel. Rock-n-roll deserved better than that. He took another deep hit on the joint and danced around the radio station. His dancing style was a cross between calisthenics and a man on fire. When the song was over he was out of breath.

"That was a song by the Beach Boys. The next song will smash your atoms." Emperor Norton glanced up at the clock and sucked in the last of the marijuana. The setting sun was turning the clouds soft pink and the twilight was almost upon him and the end of the music. The marijuana roared into his brain and all his senses buzzed. He yelled into the microphone, "We're just about finished here!" He reached down in his box and pulled out another record. His hand slapped the record on the turntable and swung the arm to just the right groove. Scratching sounds and then the guitar wailed.

...'There must be some kind of way outta here. Said the joker to the thief. There's too much confusion. I can't get no relief...
...So let us stop talkin' falsely now. The hour's getting late, hey'...

Again, he danced and played air guitar, like he did long ago as a boy, to the Jimi Hendrix song.

...'All along the watchtower, princes kept the view...
...Outside in the cold distance. A wildcat did growl. Two riders were approaching and the wind began to howl'...

At the end he dropped to his knees and played air guitar until the last musical note faded. Out of breath again, he slowly stood and staggered to the microphone. In his calmest radio voice he said, "The end of rock-n-roll." He reached down and randomly pulled out the black vinyl record from the one cardboard box, looked at it and laughed. "We're going out flaming high into the desert. Turn those radios up. Higher! Higher!"

He reached over and twisted the broadcast volume knob to max, the console hummed and sparked with intense electrical current. The monitor needles twittered on top of the red line. Every radio speaker tuned to the station crackled, ready to explode into pieces. Screaming at the top of his lungs, "Rock-n-roll forever!" The needle dropped, scratching sounds and then . . .

...'You know that it would be untrue. You know that I would be a liar, if I was to say to you, Girl, we couldn't get much higher. Come on baby, light my fire. Come on baby, light my fire, Try to set the night on fire'...

With the music blaring, he lifted the other box from his youth onto the console, blew off the dust and ripped it open. He knew some day it would come to this.

...'The time to hesitate is through. No time to wallow in the mire. Try now we can only lose. And our love become a funeral pyre. Come on baby, light my fire. Come on baby, light my fire. Try to set the night on fire, yeah'...

He looked down into the box. He could see the strange devise. The end of rock and roll. Without hesitating, he reached down and touched the green wire to the red wire.

Next day in the Center of the Universe television studio in L.A. a news cast was in progress....
"Welcome back from the break." The male newscaster smiled and his white teeth sparkled. In the control booth, the technical director toned down the white balance. "Now we turn to Sonya, our gal meteorologist."
A woman with perfect platinum hair, perfect skin, and focused smile stood before a green screen and said. "It's going to be a hot one in the center of the universe today. 114 degrees in Pasadena, Oxnard, and Rancho Cucamonga. Radiation levels will be high so take those PMX-12 tablets for sunburn. I miss the ozone layer don't you? Oh, and one other thing, we should have a terrific sunset tomorrow. The atomic explosion out in the desert last night kicked up a ton of sand and the dust cloud has drifted our way. The last rock-n-roll radio station went off the air with a bang.

"What blew up?" A newscaster asked setting her up for the joke.

Sonya looked straight into the camera and sang. "The world is alive with the sound of music."

"Oh you're so cool, Sonya."

The newscaster gave a big smile to the camera. The white balance in the control booth went crazy.

Baking

Maria Borland

Ruth was grateful for her peppermint tea. And she was grateful for the 8 hours sleep she had managed. She was grateful for her skin, which, if not glowing, appeared slightly clearer than usual. She was also grateful for the breakfast her husband had prepared for her.

She was grateful for her husband.

There was a hesitation before that last one. Five things a day. That was the plan. But why hadn't he been as quick to come to mind as the peppermint tea? She felt slightly anxious about the effort it had taken to disregard the hot shower or the sunshine or her new book, or any other possible number fives... She concluded that it must be because of the depth of her feelings. The strength and complexity of love. Yes, she thought, that must be it.

It was Autumn. A time of colour. Of bright reds and brisk walks. A time for weekend hikes and bike rides. A time when everything dies. Why shouldn't she think it? It was true, wasn't it? It wasn't a bad thing to think. Didn't she confront it every week at church? But somehow it wasn't the same. Not without the angels and the comforting handshakes and the homemade cakes in the rectory.

She was grateful for her health. Particularly now she was going to make a baby. They were going to make a baby. She couldn't help thinking of that awful expression "bun in the oven." But that's exactly what came to mind. There was something so comfortable and functional and cosy about it all that the cliché had become alarmingly true.

But back then, before they were married, she remembered how he would sit and talk at her and she would respond with such energy, and alertness, and patience. She would smile and laugh and nod enthusiastically at whatever he happened to bring up. Because they hadn't done it yet. "It" - that's what they said back then, when they were younger. And looking back, maybe that "it" was the missing factor. That "it" had been the focus. Had been the driving force and the bond. Had led them all the way to marriage.

And now there was a new "it" – an "it" that would grow inside her. An "it" that would also become less important as the years went on? No, that bit couldn't be true. This "it" would be different. That's what everyone told her anyway.

She was certainly grateful for her job. She worked in a factory, but not a dingy one. This particular factory made desserts for a high-end supermarket. She got excellent discounts. The money was good and the work, which consisted of anointing a small vanilla cheesecake with a single chocolate truffle, was remarkably easy.

She had a sudden pang of anxiety as she wondered if that was why she liked it. Because it was easy. She wondered, for what may have been the first time in her life, if she was guilty of sloth.

But deep down she knew that this couldn't be the case. She had always done exactly what was required of her.

Besides, she was incredibly efficient. She knew it. Her colleagues knew it. Her boss knew it. She worked with pace and precision. She didn't slow down in the afternoons. Yes, she relished her lunchtimes, her prawn cocktail and two finger kit-kat sandwich. But that was only because she worked so hard.

There were those who slacked. Who took an unrealistic number of toilet breaks. There were the smokers outside. But she was neither a slacker nor a smoker. She stayed at her work station. She talked politely to the people around her but never let herself become distracted. She had a rough idea of how many small chocolate truffles could be placed on how many vanilla cheesecakes in how many minutes and she rarely faltered.

She wasn't guilty of sloth at all. If anything, she was proud. That she would admit. And even in that very moment, she couldn't avoid a sudden feeling of pride. She wondered which was worse, sloth, or pride. Was there some kind of hierarchy? She would have to check.

And as she stood there, hyper-aware of her pride, her stomach started to rumble. She was hungry. So incredibly hungry that for a moment she forgot she'd had breakfast. Completely forgot about the muesli and toast her husband had lovingly prepared for her that morning. It was almost as if it had never happened.

There was nothing left inside her. She couldn't understand it. She'd only been there an hour and it was a full two and a half hours until lunchtime. She started to feel tense. Jasmine was asking her about her weekend but she couldn't recall anything about it.

"Nothing exciting" she said, and felt the knot in her belly tighten.

The cakes had never looked this way to her before. So textured. As she placed the chocolate truffle on top of the individually portioned dessert her hand lingered for a moment. She realized that she couldn't pull back. The effort was extreme. Her pride had at last been depleted.

What if she took one of the truffles from the box? No-one would notice that. No-one counted the truffles in the box, surely. There were margins for error weren't there? It wouldn't be so bad, would it? To commit such an error?

Jasmine went to the toilet in a cloud of suspicion. She'd only gone a half hour before. So Ruth put her hand into the box and took out two truffles. As she placed one of them onto the cake, she put the other in her mouth.

It was done. The chocolate truffle had been taken. It had already begun to melt. There was nothing anyone could do about it now. So what if she enjoyed it? In practical terms that would not increase her crime. If this one truffle, that was now in her mouth, had already deprived the company of a few pence, what more harm could she do? What good would a sudden effort of will or silent sacrifice do anyone? Nothing at all. She gave into the bitter-sweet softness. She enjoyed it. More than she'd enjoyed the peppermint tea or the breakfast or.... She tried not to think anymore.

"I'm just going to the toilet" she said and excused herself.

She walked down the long corridor behind the main floor. She dawdled a little by the stock cupboard. She looked out of the one square window and watched the smokers taking their deep indulgent breaths.

At the end of the corridor she turned left, away from the toilet and towards the admin room where Mark sat at his desk, scribbling. She coughed. He looked up.

"Oh. Hi!"

Mark smiled.

"Sorry. I was just on my way to the toilet and I thought I'd say hello"

Mark had fancied her for over a year.

"I stole one of the truffles" she confessed

"Did you?"

"I just took it out of the box and put it in my mouth"

"Why did you do that?"

"I don't know. I just couldn't stop myself. I mean I just had this sudden craving. And then I took it, and it was so good. In fact it may be the best thing I've ever tasted, and then I said I wanted to go to the toilet but actually I didn't at all, actually I just wanted to walk down the corridor. To wander leisurely down the corridor. And look out of the window. And then, when I got to the end of the corridor I suddenly wanted to come down here. I wanted to come into your room...and....and..."

*****

She walked back down the corridor, a little warmer now. Somewhat dazed. She almost veered into Aiden, the estates manager. She went to her work station and saw that Jasmine had returned.

"Baking"

"What?"

"That's what we did. At the weekend. My husband and I. We baked a cake. I remember now."

The Dance

Trevor Maynard
Adapted from the journals
of RH Cunningham

With an intoxicated air of masculine pride, vigour, and youthful smugness, Dex Denby and I returned from our shopping trip loaded with our fashion haul: silver grey, 22-inch width, Oxford Bag trousers, light blue shirts, serge blazers with brass buttons... very smart; and then there were the 'winkle picker' shoes tapering to a fine, shiny point, all the better to cut a dashing rug on the dance floor. Admittedly Dex was a bit of a 'gigolo' with the women, whilst I was still far too shy and naive. Still, I would forever be indebted to Dex: It was he who first introduced me to ballroom dancing, which was to become both my lifelong passion, and my great comfort.

He also introduced me to Cathy, one of his exes. In fact, it was probably quite hard to find any girl that Dex had not had, at least, his eye on. I was not, however, inexperienced. Maria, eight years my senior, had taken care of that, showing me the basics, and more; although she was only ever a 'go to', and of course, though I didn't realise it at the time, I was not her only lover. As I look back on my life, I am glad that she was older, and I consider myself fortunate to have met her. For many of my contemporaries, acquiring sexual experience was fraught with difficulties and embarrassing setbacks, especially with those of the same age. On every level it was 'risky': putting the 'cart before the horse', leading, for some, to heartache and divorce further down the line.

Cathy, however, was very different, we would go on long, romantic country walks, and although the subject was never broached directly, I would discover her relationship with Dex had prematurely ended because of his increasingly heavy drinking and abusive behaviour. It seemed while I got to see the gregarious, amicable, Dex, more often than not she got the side that left punch marks on her arms, foul words ringing in her ears, and tears running down her pretty cheeks. Whilst I was not yet as good a dancer as Dex, I adored Cathy and literally swooned around her: she was my first real love. Emotionally, however, I knew I had a lot more growing up to do, because before long my romantic eyes clouded over with jealousy and possessiveness, as I discovered my own unexpected anger if another man so much as looked at her. I managed to keep my outbursts in check, but I'd learnt a very important lesson about myself.

Having a night out at The Kursaal Ballroom in Southend-on-Sea was a special treat, and was well worth the one shilling and sixpence return, plus the two shilling, eight pence entrance fee. A fair fee in those days; it was 1937. By now I had a decent job as a petrol tanker driver's mate, delivering up to 2,500 gallons to Cromer and the like. By chance, or luck, the tanker driver I was with was another 'ladies' man, but the advantage I gained from this period was one of work experience as I often had to drive the truck so that he could sleep off the night before! The cue for me to take over would be he'd often miss first gear on a steep hill, and I'd have to jump out with a big wooden 'chuck' to stop our tanker rolling back down the hill. Wealdon, the driver, regaled me throughout with his torrid tales of sexual conquests, and the advantages of being on the road; he visited women in Cromer, Chelmsford, and Tilbury, as well as his own 'sweet strife' back in the East End of London. Experiences from all quarters of my life were piling up: I was in my prime, life was good. At the age of 26, whilst doing my favourite dance, the slow Foxtrot, I eventually met the beautiful woman who would become my wife.

Most of the young men in my circle of friends went out to drink of an evening, then buoyed up with Dutch courage, would look to muscle in on women for the last Waltz. Maybe this appealed to one or two girls, but it would often lead to trouble and an old-style bar brawl. I, on the other hand, preferred to turn up early, when mostly only women occupied the dance floor, expertly partnering each other for the various popular ballroom dances of that time; then, I was able to get a good partner who had come to dance seriously. This way, I would learn: not only new steps but also new dances from them. I also learnt about the advantages of being sober at the end of the evening, and so shandy became my drink of choice, for a while. This also often left me as the designated driver, though I never actually had a car myself.

So, there were trips to Canvey, when the tide was favourable, and up to Chelmsford, and down to Southend to either dance, or play soccer, or frequently both as the dances were often fundraisers for the football. These were some of the thrilling times I would get my chance to be out on the open road.

One such occasion came during a Whitsun' Monday outing to Maldon, in a two seater Morris Oxford with a dodgy seat. It was a glorious day, brilliant sunshine, country pubs, time by the muddy banks of the River Crouch, in the long grass with a couple of girls and my mate Todd Hooper. Todd was serious about his girl, and it made me nervous to see the raw arduousness in his eyes. I knew the problems, and jealousy this could bring up; sure enough, as the sun fell and reddened the sky, so another scotch, and another scotch darkened his mood. Maybe his girl wasn't as serious on Todd, but whatever the reason, Todd now wanted to drive, it was his car, and I was relegated to the back space with my girl, not an unpleasant experience, I must admit. By now it was dark, no streetlights like modern times, and Todd cut into the bends, only just on the edge of controlling each swerve. Thunderously silent, shoulders rigid, Todd's hands gripped fiercely on the wheel, while his girl had shrunken deep into her seat, pretending to be asleep. It was a terrifying journey which, inevitably, soon came to it's tragic end.

The crash happened shortly before 11pm.

My girl and I were thrown clear into the bracken, the Morris Oxford eventually stopped upside down in a ditch. I can still remember as if it was yesterday how clear the sky was that night, and full of stars, the air crisp and sharp, perfect to carry the screams of Todd's girl, and Todd's own plaintive moaning. I managed to pull the girl free, but Todd was severely trapped beneath the steering wheel, conscious but complaining of excruciating pain in his stomach. The ambulance arrived and Todd was rushed away somewhere, while the girls and I were taken to a local casualty.

Fortunately, Todd's girl had only a broken arm, my girl and I were only suffering minor cuts and bruising; we were shocked, but otherwise ok. By the next morning, however, we had to deal with the devastating news that Todd had passed away. It fell to me, or rather I decided to take responsibility, to inform Todd's parents he'd died.

For as long as I could remember, at that age, it felt as though war in Europe was always on the horizon; it once again became a reality when it reared its ugly head during 1939. I was newly married by now, and my lorry, or more specifically, me as its' driver, were commandeered by the army to deliver food, taking me away on short notice from my young wife, and our new-born son. We had met through our love of ballroom dancing, and we'd progressed from... "may I ask you for a dance" and "thank you very much" to proper courtship -

once she'd dumped her then boyfriend- to our engagement and marriage.

Now though, we were separated by the darkly gathered clouds of war. The army didn't tell us where or for how long I was going, but it did give me a taster of army life which I did not enjoy, for in all but name, we were now in uniform. After another six months, the army department called me, and every other able young man, to make it official, it was a time of forced conscription, but, I felt there was no way I wanted to go into khaki, so I took a huge, naive, gamble and told a white lie, saying my father and uncle were ex-navy, and therefore that was the service I wanted to serve with. It paid off, and I was 'in the Navy'.

However, I soon found out there is no experience more sickening, or terrifying, than the cramped living conditions below the deck of a warship during violent seas with over a thousand men vomiting... fear penetrating every fibre of our beings, the 'knowing' that death is coming to you, or your shipmates, or your loved ones back home.

My wife and I had a second child, a little girl, in 1942, but there was precious little leave during the duration of the war, and by the time I properly met my daughter, she was already three years old. Each time I came home it was painfully clear that the relative innocence of life before was gone, and the tragedy of battle took its toll not just in causalities of life, but also on relationships back home. My wife and I became estranged. Most servicemen and I knew only of our own experiences in war, not of the emotional and mental battles fought back home. We were ill equipped to deal with the fallout, and while faded black and white photographs showed my wife and family celebrating VE day at a street party in England, I was on board a ship sailing to the Pacific, where three months later, we visited Nagasaki, seeing first hand that new phase in humanity's evolution, the nuclear age.

Following the war, and especially after my wife's sudden, inexplicable death in 1947, I did not have the emotional ability to return home. Physically, yes, at times, I was at home, with my two young children, but my absence was always pending, and in the end, I could only leave them in the care of my two spinster sisters. The navy had become my home, my family, and sadly as it may seem, it is to the Navy that I will always be grateful for helping me in my hour of tragedy, and for giving me the comfort I felt I could find nowhere else.

To be alone with my tortured thoughts seemed unbearable, but the distraction of activity, purpose, and shipmates to cushion the blow, I, perhaps mistakenly, felt I was able get through the pain. One day I would have to face reality alone, be responsible for my family, the parent for my children; but for now, I simply wasn't ready to cope with it.

Where one war ends, another is always waiting to begin. It was the Korean War next, 1950. I

was on HMS Belfast as we sailed up the Yellow River on a typical mission. Shells bombarded a shore base, and maybe stopped a few Chinese soldiers being smuggled in on small boats. From our position on the river, we sometimes watched American Napalm bombs pound against the hillside catacombs, scorching out the enemy. Once, such is the gallows humour of war, we found a US pilot shot down by enemy flak, but we refused to hand him back to the Yanks until they exchanged him for a cargo of ice cream.

Getting injured, a leg-burn in 1951, meant I had to leave the Royal Navy. After being de-mobbed from the service, I once again appealed to the good nature of my sisters and they agreed to continue raising my children. I became a workaholic on merchant ships for the next two years, all my money going back to fund a new life that I hoped was coming.

I believed I'd done my duty and faced responsibility: when Todd died and when war came, but for my family, my children, I realise I hadn't faced responsibility, not since 1940; for even when I returned, to driving long haul lorries, I was spending many, too many, nights away. It was not for another two years later that I finally 'came home' from the war.

In my later years, settled and happy with my second wife, and being a grandfather, I began to write journals, in an attempt, to make sense of the thoughts and experiences of my past.

I started back with my childhood, in the tenements of Glasgow, where, from aged 6, it was my job to sluice through the single toilet shared by four families. The place where my drunken, gambling, docker father, beat us; where, the schools were factions of 'Proddy' and 'Papist'.
I then moved on to my time in Essex, where we, my mother and sisters, essentially escaped that Old Holborn smoking tyrant, at least until his final dying years. Next, I looked at key events through my formative years, Dex, Wealdon, and Todd, and finally my time during the wars, my first wife, and my children.

Through it all, there was always the dancing, the Foxtrot, the Rumba, and the Cha Cha Cha. After yet another spell back at sea, but one where I had swapped my sailor's whites for those of the Chief Steward on an Ocean liner, I married again, in 1968. For 37 years we were together, something completely unexpected when you marry at 58 years old.

My hand-written notebooks, impossible to read by many, have been transcribed, where legible enough, first by my son, and now with somewhat more artistic flair, by my grandson.

This is a tale of one human life, seen through human eyes, sometimes fortunate, sometimes unfortunate, neither perfect nor imperfect; it simply was, and is.

From the Journals of Robert Hamilton Cunningham (1911-2006): Transcribed and edited by Robert Frederick Hamilton (2015): Written by Trevor Maynard (2017).

Biographies

SANDY NORRIS
No Going Back

Sandy is the winner of the RH Cunningham Memorial Short Story Prize for 2017

She is a retired English teacher turned writer. In 2005 her children's novel: *Run Away to Danger* was published by the National Maritime Museum but more recently she has begun to write for an adult audience and has completed two novels, both of which have garnered some agent interest, although neither has yet found a publisher.

She is now researching a third novel about the spitfire women in World War Two.

Israela Margalit
Too Much

Israela Margalit is an award-winning
writer, playwright, and concert pianist.
Her credits include the Gold Medal New
York Film & TV Festival, Two NEA Media
Awards, an Emmy Nomination, finalist
the Long Island Film Festival, finalist the
Glimmer Train Press Short Fiction
Competition, Best Play Honorary
Mention the New York 15-minute Play
Festival, Best Production New York MIT
Festival, an Ovation-recommendation
LA, and Best CD the British Music
Industry Awards

Belinda DuPret
When Food Kills

UK Born Linda DuPret comes from a
vaguely showbiz family and describes
herself as a secondary-modern dropout,
who's somehow earned a living by writing.
She's been a DJ; music promoter;
freelance journalist; food writer and a TV
Reporter, and worked in New Zealand,
France, England, Australia and the USA.
Now she's a happily born-again hippie
living back in the UK. All people (plus
wine and food) in this story exist but are
innocent of any crime.

Lynne Zotalis
True North

Lynne is a published author and poet practicing peace journalism through the Loft Literary Society in Minneapolis, MN being a member in their Peace and Social Justice Writer's Group.

Environmental activism is pursued through organizations dedicated to managing and prohibiting silica sand mining as well as protecting our water resources thereby ensuring a verdant planet for generations. Books written and contributed to by Lynne are available through online retailers.

Michael McLaughlin
The Death of Rock 'n' Roll

Michael was the founder, producer, and actor with an improvisational comedy troupe in Sacramento, California for 20 years. He has appeared in films, television, and yes, radio.

He has had short stories appeared in periodicals around the world. In 2005 he escaped to Ajijic, Mexico to write and live. You should too. Presently he is producer and director of a benefit lip sync show (the largest and longest running show in the world!) for the city's theater...

Maria Borland
Baking

Originally from London, Maria Borland studied
English Literature at Sheffield and Playwriting
at Goldsmiths before completing a PGCE and
working full time as a teacher. Since then, she
has taught in a variety of places, from Derby
and Cambridge in the UK to South Korea and
Budapest. She currently lives and works in
Bogota, Colombia, where she teaches
literature at an international school.

Trevor Maynard
The Dance

Poet, playwright, writer and editor, Trevor Maynard's latest collection of poetry is *Grey Sun Dark Moon*. He is the managing editor of *The Poetic Bond* series of international poetry anthologies, which so far have published the work of over 130 poets. The seventh volume of *The Poetic Bond* will be published in Autumn 2017. He directed and produced ten of his own plays, six of which have been published, including four in the collection *Four Truths*. He has had short stories published in several international magazines. He has also edited *Echoes in the Earth*, the latest collection of poetry from award winning Indian poet Pushpita Awasthi.

Robert Hamilton Cunningham
1911-2006

1911 – Born, East End of London, Moved to Glasgow

1912 – Moved to Essex in 1927, finding work as a drivers' mate. Early 1930's, keen amateur footballer, and ballroom dancer, meeting his wife to be, Vera, in 1936.

1937 – Married Vera Hasler

1938 – Birth of first child, Robert Frederick

1939 – World War II; called up to the Army, but decides to join the Navy instead

1940-1942 - Serves on HMS Swiftsure

1942 – Birth of second child, Christine Eleanor

1945 – Part of the flotilla where Japan signed their surrender after nuclear bombs dropped on Hiroshima and Nagasaki ended WW2

1947 – His wife Vera, loses her life while swimming of the coast of Southend-on-Sea

1947 – returns to the Navy, leaving his sisters Jessie and Ellen to look after his children.

1950 – On HMS Belfast in Korea

1951 – Demobbed after injury, works on ships

1953 – Sisters emigrate to Australia as £10 Poms,

1960 – Robert Frederick marries Patricia Laver,

1961 - Christine marries Brian Maynard
RH returns to sea, as a Chief Steward on Ocean liners

1963 - Grandson Trevor Brian Maynard born
1966 – Grandson David Michael Maynard born
1968 - Marries Jean Strauss
1968 - Works for Pickfords, then for as a taxi
         driver for AC Cabs for many years
1971 - Grandson Andrew Cunningham born

Throughout the seventies, eighties, and nineties, he and his "Wee Jeanie" danced, and taught, ballroom dancing; he became social secretary of Southend-Conservative Club.

He once told me, "you should be a socialist when you are young and idealistic, but a conservative when you grow older and realistic." He became life president of Southend Conservative Club in 2000, though it would seem, I, am still young and idealistic enough to remain a socialist.

2006, shortly before his 95th birthday, and still dancing, RH passes away in Southend. A bench bearing his name looks out over Southend Pier. It is believed by some, he has been reincarnated as a seagull and often hovers on the breeze over the cliffs.

Writing "The Dance"

In the 1980's, during his 'seventies, my grandfather began to pen his memoirs in a series of handwritten notebooks. This was not a deliberate attempt at a coherent memoir, rather a process of wanting to put down his thoughts and to revisit his life, both to reflect, and to pass on. The results produce a fascinating look into the past, from a personal perspective, as well as the reflections of man whose life was not always easy. They were initially transcribed by his son, Robert Frederick Cunningham for his Degree dissertation on the history of the Cunningham family, which was later published privately. Taking both my uncle's book, and my grandfather's notes, as well as some artistic license, the short story included in this collection, seeks to capture the spirit of his life. I am also grateful to my wife, Jo, for her editing of my manuscript, helping to bring my grandfather's story to life.

Three
Flash Fiction
Stories

Insomnia
© *GK Grieve*

Lately I've been waking up in the middle of the night. Not in a cold sweat. Not from a bad dream. Not, it seems, for any physical reason. One minute, I am asleep, the next I am awake. Sometimes I lay, without moving, for an hour. I stare at the ceiling; there are shadows from the bare branches of the trees, and I imagine they make shapes, but it is only my delusion. I think it is an excuse to explain my insomnia. There must be a ghost. Or an alien. Something extraordinary to explain this mundane sleeplessness.

I asked a doctor. Not a psychotherapist, or a psychologist, or even a psychiatrist; just a regular General Practitioner. She wrote a prescription for Diazepam. This is a drug I have heard of, but not good things. It is for depression, or at the very least anxiety, and I do not feel either of these, or feel I have any degree of such conditions. So, I decided not to take them.

"Just take the goddam pills," my wife said, the frustration and irritation clear in her voice. It was four in the morning, and my waking had woken her, again. She turned onto her side, taking most of the duvet with her. My legs felt cold. The hairs on my arms, and the back of my neck, were standing on end. There was a bead of sweat. I took the pills. I never woke again.

A Smile of a Thousand Stars
© *Neetu Malik*

Daddy took me by the hand as we walked through a park. I hadn't told him how bruised I was from a friendship fallen apart. How does one explain hurt feelings when your best friend ditches you and leaves you standing on the wayside, and you feel as though you weren't good enough?

I guess daddy didn't need the words to know the pain I felt. He didn't ask; I didn't tell. His strong hand transferred to mine the soothing balm of affection and the understanding of unspoken pain.

He lifted and sat me on a swing, pushing me high up to feel the butterflies in my stomach, the blue sky coming closer as I rose higher with every push.

We stopped for my favorite pistachio ice cream on the way back home. His eyes twinkled like a thousand stars as he sat across me, their beam radiating to my soul. I smiled.

Today, we are walking together again. Forty years later, he is holding my hand and I have tears in my eyes and sorrow in my soul. He says nothing. Neither do I. He leans on a walking stick with his free hand. The tight, warm hold of his other hand on mine tells me he understands. We stop at Joe's Café by Central Park. I get my black coffee, he his sweet tea with milk. He smiles his smile of a thousand stars at me. I return the beam of love.

My nine-year-old grand-daughter, Sophia, also has a very active imagination; it is one my grandfather, RH Cunningham, a keen amateur footballer, and a bit of a storyteller himself, would have appreciated.

Emma, The Football Fairy.
© *Sophia Keech*

The New Fairy
Emma was a football fairy. Football, and football fairies, weren't very popular in Fairyland. Emma was a newcomer to Fairyland. Not one fairy welcomed her, or helped her build her house, so she had to build it all on her own! Emma was really tired afterwards.

The Big Announcement
As she was making her tea one morning, Emma heard, on the Fairyland loudspeaker, that there was to be a sports tournament, including football! Just as she was celebrating the possibility that she would now get the opportunity to meet new fairies, and maybe get a chance to show everyone her football skills, there was a knock at the door. Another football fairy was asking whether she was doing the football competition. Emma said YES!

The Big Day
It had finally come, the Big Day! Emma was so excited; she quickly got into her football kit. The game started, her team was winning, but oh no, another team player had hit the ball too hard, and too high! She couldn't see what Emma could see as the ball zoomed into a tree! Emma flew as fast as her wings would carry her! Quickly, she saved the bird's eggs as they fell, out of their nest. Everyone in Fairyland cheered. Well done Emma, the Football Fairy!

Two poems
In Memoriam

cha cha cha

there is one less person in the world today
one less person to dance, to sing,
to greet the guests, to make the sandwiches
to talk about the young ones, to play the host
to clean the glasses with paper not cloth

there is one less person in the world today
to sip a Courvoisier
to shake my hand

one less person to remember the horror of war
the fear, the indignity, the pain,
one less person who *endured*
to save us all

but yet, as the saying goes,
a glass half empty is a glass half full

there are a thousand more memories in the world today
recollections of wise words and knowledge,
of experience, of times of happiness and joy
of places far and wide, harbours and oceans and seas,
memories of toys and mechanicals made of tin
presents from the four corners of the world
tales and stories from around the globe
but then always back to England
and the words often said

"the most important thing is family"
"i'm so glad to have you all here"
"i have been lucky in my life"

there are thousands of gifts of reminiscence to enjoy
of showing the young ones how to dance
the paso doblé, the samba, the waltz,
the foxtrot, the rumba and the cha cha cha
memories of the sharp dresser, the white tuxedo, the bow
        tie
remembrance of holidays abroad and at home,
of castanets and maracas,
of beach hut summers and swimming in the North Sea
of lolly stick battles and conker competitions
of looking up through the waves and being pulled into
        strong arms

there are a thousand gifts of memory
born today and every day
of daily walks along the cliffs looking out to the sea
of the time when a stranger was invited to a wedding to
        make fourteen
of Hogmanay and kilts, of coal brought for the new year

so many more gifts given to everyone here
to keep, to cherish, to be constant in thought
always in our hearts we will dance with you,
the paso doblé, the samba, the waltz,
the foxtrot, the rumba, the cha cha cha
the foxtrot, the rumba, and the cha cha cha

In Memory of RH Cunningham 1911-2006

Trevor Maynard (2006)

114

"Tuesday"

Of a Tuesday
We would reside
Upon the evening
At the Big White House, on the corner

There, as the notes of a piano
Drifted from hand, to string, to air
In the kitchen, there would stand
Wee Jeanie, with her Bob

Little Davey, and Trevor (that's me)
Awaited the signal for bed
Our dapper grandparents, always smiling
Discussed a dance, or a piece of music
Or spoke, ever fondly, of Scotland
Milk was always from a 'beaker'
Never a mug

Of a Tuesday
On New Years' Eve
When Hogmanay set in
Nanny Jean wore a paper crown
Perched, precariously
In gravity defying, tall black hair
Always black, and with all arms linked
In her soft Ayrshire accent, never to fade
Sang of "old Acquaintance..."

*

Of a Tuesday
I would sometimes pick up the phone
Never often enough, I must admit
The conversation would be brief
But would mean the world
"How're you and the family?" She would ask
"Look forward to seeing you soon!"
"Bye, bye, darling, thanks for calling." She
would end

These later years, when, as a seagull
My grandfather, her Bob, would hover
And fly along the cliffs and out to sea
New voices came into her world
The families of her grandchildren grew
Great grandchildren were born
Great-great grandchildren arrived
Wee Jeanie loved every wee one of us

She made all children smile
She never judged and always supported
She encouraged and showed pride
And usually, if you were 'lucky'
She supplied mini-colas, toffees, and Kit-Kats
And gave up a fridge magnet or two

Of a Tuesday
The last note played
Upon the morning
At the Big White House, on the corner

Where we last visited Nanny Jean
Her hands, warm and soft
Her eyes smiling, always happy to see us
But happier still, to see her Bob
She recalled their life of dancing
The waltz, the quick-step, the cha-cha-cha
And she asked that on this day
Here, at this place, there should be no black
That we too should recall
And celebrate one last waltz with her

In memory of Jean Ramsay Cunningham 1927 – 2016

Trevor Maynard (2016)

118

The Poetic Bond

The Poetic Bond series of poetry anthologies is now in its seventh year and has published over 130 poets from 17 countries.

The Poetic Bond VII will be published in November 2017

What makes a poetic bond?

The process of selecting poems for publishing *The Poetic Bond* series is unlike any other in that there is no set plan as to what will be published. It depends on the themes which emerge from the pool of work submitted, or to put it another way, the poetic energy which comes together at this certain time and place. Where themes emerge, patterns of energy harmonize, form bonds, connections, and these in turn lead to interconnected chapters, and the creation of a holistic volume, deeply connected with humanity, nature, and the universe.

The Poetic Bond VI (2016)

ISBN-10 : 1539334686
ISBN 13 : 978-1539334682

Featuring

Christine Anderes (USA) : *The Ossurary of James / The Unquiet Heart*

Pushpita Awasthi (India) : *In My Heart of H-earts / Words in the Dark*

Rebecca Behar (France) : *Procession*

Betty Bleen (USA) : *Grandma's Jesus / The Cutting Edge*

Diane Burrow (UK) : *Speechless / Take a Look at the Hills*

George Carter (UK) : *When I got there*

Diane Colette (USA) : *Fields of Asphodel*

Ian Colville (UK) : *A Cliché for our Time / Ploughing*

William DiBenedetto (USA) : *time comes uninvited / 7-May-1915*

Belinda DuPret (UK) : *Isobel*

Amanda Eakin (USA) : *The Broken Repairman*

Madalana Fine (UK) : *Lost letter From Love*

Bonnie Flach (USA) : *At the Crossroads*

GK Grieve (UK) : *The Final Moment Before the Death of Swans / Addict*

Robin Hislop (UK) : *Tenochitian / In Bed*

Rowland Hughes (UK) : *Lemon Soap / A Valley Funeral*

Wendy Joseph (USA) : *This is America / In My House, There are Books / When the Water Rises*

Jill Angel Langlois (USA) : *If the Wind Blows / I Remember Silence*

Lawrence W. Lee (USA) : *Cynic / Still Life*

Carey Link (USA) : *Blur Distinctions*

Kwai Chee Low (Malaysia) : *Cold Winter, Warm Heart*

Neetu Malik (USA) : *dancers / The Pianist / Wanderer*

Trevor Maynard (UK) : *take flight / crushed*

Michael Melichov (Israel) : *Cards*

Miklos Mezosi (Hungary) : *An Iamblified Inquiry*

Linda Mills (USA) : *Abide / Winter Seep*

Greg Mooney (USA):*Insecurities* **Marli Merker Moreira (Brazil)**:*Drifters*

Judith Neale (Canada) : *One Cleft Moon*

Hongvan Nguyen (USA) : *Becoming*

Bonnie Roberts (USA) : *Cautionary Steps of Love*

George C. Robertson (UK) : *Engraved / A Burning Desire*

Joseph J. Simmons (USA):*1914* **Nana Tokatli (Greece)**:*Wheat Fields*

Swaizi Vaughan (USA) : *E-Turn Next Left Dead IN / Prepubescent*

Will Walsh (USA) : *Onion Creek, Utah / As I live and breathe / Evolution*

Cigeng Zhang (China) : *Hey, Starling / Special Reunion / Wa Lan / One-line Tide*

The Poetic Bond V (2015)

ISBN-10: 1517783801
IS ISBN-13: 978-1517783808

<u>Featuring</u>
Amanda Valerie Judd (USA): Poetry
Belinda Dupret (UK): Ginervra da Benci
Betty Bleen (USA): A Different Mourning
Bonnie Flach (USA): Harbor Night Songs / Realization
Bonnie Roberts (USA): Road Sings.../In Vacation Bible School...
Brian McCully (Australia): The Journey of H'won
Caroline Glen (Australia): Together / Peach Tree
Christine Anderes (USA): Never Sure / Somewhere else...
Cigeng Zhang (China): At 8 'clock / Still For You /
The Moon, The Poet
Claire Mikkelsen (USA): Moanin' the Blues
Clark Cook (Canada): An Autumn Journey / Reluctant Travellers
Diane Wend (UK): Sleek in the Sun
Rhona Davidson (UK): Not Just a False Alarm / Waiting / Stuck
Frances Ayers (USA): Well Fought Tears
Freddie Ostrovskis (UK): The Waiting Tree
Gilbert A. Franke (USA): Music, Love and Memories /
Promises From A Rose Garden
GK Grieve (UK): Jessica / Ian Colville (UK): Group-think
James Sutton (USA): Lenny Bruce Presents ... J.b
Jill Angel Langlois (USA): Botanical Garden /
Joseph Simmons (USA): Iostring / Pete Soron (UK): For Love
Julie Clark (UK): A Babbling Stream / Behold the New Jerusalem
Kewayne Wadley (USA): Together / Peach Tree
Leander Seddon (Australia): Bird of Paradise,
Linda Mills (USA): Gone Sound / Sleepy Dragon
Marli Merker Moreira (Brazil): Behind Bars
Nana Tokatli (Greece): The white carpet / an empty space
Neetu Malik (USA): The Cobwebs / A walk in the rain / Limbo
Pushpita Awasthi (Netherlands): Cecile / Synonym of Love
RH Peat (USA): Flying Fingers / The Chinese Restaurant
Robin Ouzman Hislop (UK): A Split Second Later's Late / The Split
Sonia Kilvington (Cyprus): Wild Montana / Object of Desire
Trevor Maynard (UK): The Grey Sun / Human
Wendy Joseph (USA) Never Sure / Somewhere else...
William diBenedetto (USA): wow they have

The Poetic Bond IV (2014)

ISBN-10: 1503034526
ISBN-13: 978-1503034525

<u>Featuring</u>
Christine Anderes *(USA): Illumination*
Mark Beechill *(UK): Wrangle*
Scott Pendragon Black *(USA) : Past*
Rosalind Brenner *(USA): The Night Jesus Spoke;*
Art Show; Meeting Mother
Clark Cook *(Canada) : Another Kind of Sunset*
*, ***Catherine DeWolf** *(USA) : Tantrum*
William DiBenedetto *(USA) : 3am overdraft blues*
Belinda Dupret *(UK) : The Scent of Trees*
Bonnie J. Flach *(US) : Najavo Sand Painter*
G A. Franke *(USA) : Reflections on the Sea*
Ingrid Gjelsvik *(Norway) : no frame*
the floe inside the bookcases;
GK Grieve *(UK): Dark Soul*
Peter Hagen *(Norway) : To Set A Big Cry Free*
Seamus Harrington *(Eire) : Free Downloads; Open Day*
Diane Jardel *(Eire) : Alzheimer Blues I & II -*
"It's OK" - " I am here my love"
Trevor Maynard *(UK) : the earthmovers; Clarity*
Clare Mikkelsen *(USA) : A New Bottom Line / Tiny Banker*
Jude Neale *(Canada) Poe: The Arrangement*
Hongvan Nguyen *(USA) : Singers*
RH Peat *(USA) : At The Cost of Others' Eyes;*
Crows in the Snow
Patricia Pfahl *(Canada) : How To Love A Woman;*
The Hammock; Obsidian
Bonnie Roberts *(USA) : Daddy, Who Cut The Moon In Half;*
Swimming Home To Myself
Sayed H. Rohani *(Afghanistan) : Tales of Love*
Peter Alan Soron *(UK) : Click here to make a million*
Cigeng Zhang *(China) : What was left*

The Poetic Bond III (2013)

ISBN-10: 1492384194
ISBN-13: 978-1492384199

Featuring

Christine Anderes (New York, USA) : *Migration; The Moon Rides High In The Sky* / **Graham Bates** (Christchurch, New Zealand) : *Rapture; Jazz Intelligence* / **Mark Beechill** (Kent, UK) : *Back to Work*
Rebecca Behar (Paris, France) :*About Turner's Paintings of Venice I & II*
Nikki Bennett (Merseyside, UK) : *Hinge Cradled in its Own Cap; Thicker Skin* / **Rosalind Brenner** (New York, USA) : *God's Rebuke*
BJ Brown (Connecticut, USA) : *Edu-Can't Cry Sis*
Ian Colville (Bedfordshire, UK) : *Waiting Bridge* / *The History of the Clothes Line in Medieval Europe* / **Clark Cook** (British Columbia, Canada) : *Stopping Trains* / **William DiBenedetto** (Seattle, US) : *Triton Beach; Angelo's Hat* / **Sam Doctors** (California, USA) : *A Brindled Cast; A Supine Oak; In Praise of Stone Fences*
Belinda Dupret (West Sussex, UK) : *The Scent of Honey*
Sumita Dutta (Chennai, India) : *Her Flight*
Nina Floreteng (Haninge, Sweden) : *The Shadow*
Louise Francois (Middlesex, UK) : *Tomato 'Trumpet Red'*
Gilbert A Franke (Texas, USA) : *Chief Joseph*
GK Grieve (London, UK) : *The Anniversary*
Seamus Harrington (Cork, Eire) : *The Hunter*
Scott Hastie (Hertfordshire, UK) : *Life Collects*
James Higgins (Oregon, USA) : *Family Trait; Party Manners*
Robin Ouzman Hsilop (South Yorkshire, UK) : *Red Butterflies / From Here To Silence* / **Diane Jardel** (Eire) : *Light and Shade*
Mark L Levinson (Israel) : *The Book; The Agent*
Carey Link (Alabama, USA) : *Where Am I?* / **Trevor Maynard** (Surrey, UK) : *Beyond The Writing On The Wall; The Chattering Ants*
Mermie (UK) : *Eggshells; The Eve Of Independence*
Simon Miller (Kent, UK) : *Tingling Point* / **Linda Mills** (Oregon, USA) : *A Cloud of Butterflies; Coal Taking* / **Marli Merker Moreira** (Brazil) : *Vacant Eyes* / **Christine Pearson** (Maryland, USA) : *I DIDN'T KNOW I LOVED* / **RH Peat** (California, USA) : *Forgotten Embroidery*
Bonnie Roberts (Alabama, USA) *Spirit Animal; God's Opposable Thumb Leaves Me Feeling Uncomforted*
Niek Satjin (Amsterdam, Holland) : *alles fängt an mit der Neugier* / **Sharla Lee Shults** (Georgia, USA) : *Messages in the Wind*
Pete Soron (UK)*: Beard* / **Charles Thielman** (Chicago, USA) : *Faith in the Ruins* / **Cigeng Zhang** (China) *Drunk Smile*

The Poetic Bond II (2012)

ISBN-10: 1480209732
ISBN-13: 978-1480209732

Featuring

Christine Anderes (New York, USA) : *The Power Of Circles*
Frances Ayers (New York, USA) : *Grief Has No Hold*
Graham Bates (Christchurch, New Zealand) : *Untitled*
Rebecca Behar (Paris, France) : *The Tradition Man*
JE Bird (Surrey, UK) : *Part of the Process*
Lewis Bosworth (Wisconsin, USA) : *On Billy; Coloring Kids*
Jessie Brown (Massachusetts, USA) : *Lucy Clifton Rising in the Northern Sky;*
Love ; Novenas / **Robert Campion** (Surrey, UK) : *Grey*
Tim Coburn (Cumbria, UK) : *My Toybox was my treasure*
Ian Colville (Bedfordshire, UK) : *Timed Out*
James Darcy (Hampshire, UK) : *Alone* / **Sam Doctors** (California, USA) : *A*
Time Suspended / **Belinda DuPret** (West Sussex, UK) : *Fruitful*
Nina Floreteng (Haninge, Sweden) : *Spring of Awakening*
Gilbert A Franke (Texas, USA) : *The Stocking Cap*
William Gregory (Kent, UK) : *The Unseen*
Robin Ouzman Hislop (South Yorkshire, UK) : *Far from Equilibrium*
Rachel Z Ikins (New York, USA) : *Beneath a Saturn Sky*
Romi Jain (Jaipur, India) : *Would you come to me?*
Diane Jardel (Eire): *Grass* / **Cathriona Lafferty** (Spain) : *A Love in Chains*
John Lambremont Snr (Louisiana, USA) : *To My Octogenarian*
Frieda W Landau (Florida, USA) : *When the Revolution was Young*
Naomi Madelin (Bristol, UK) : *When you meet me*
Trevor Maynard (UK): *Gently, I walk the water's edge; My love is like the ocean*
Marli Merker Moreira (Brazil) : *First Kiss*
Miklos Mezosi (Budapest, Hungary) : *Farewell! Do spend thy time and money*
well! / **Linda Mills** (Oregon, USA) : *From My Eye*
Robert Prattico (Massachusetts, USA) : *Poetry is Dead*
Nancy Pritchard (Missouri, USA) : *Dreaming in an Alley; Allusions*
Bonnie Roberts (Alabama, USA) : *In Lieu of Flowers*
Nancy Scott (New Jersey, USA) *The Poor Man's Bride*
Sharla Lee Shults (Georgia, USA) : *Echoes in Wartime*
Peter Alan Soron (not disclosed) : *in quietness and green*
Antony Taylor (Texas, USA) : *The Barber*
Janet Gell Thompson (Derbyshire, UK) : *Little Lacemakers*
Tom Watts (Bristol, UK) : *On Visiting El Castellon*
Ann Widdicor (Norway) : *Spent Aquilegia*
Michaelle Yarborough (North Carolina, USA): *Tank*

The Poetic Bond (2011)

ISBN (10) 1466498412
ISBN (13) 978-1466498419

Featuring

George Chijioke Amadi (Lagos, Nigeria) : *A Wife's Neck Saved*
Graham Bates (Christchurch, New Zealand) : *Touch*
Marguerite Guzman Bouvard (Massachusetts, USA) : *Bougainvillea; Invisible* / **Dan Brook** (California, USA) : *November Ninth*
Bonnie Gail Carter (Indiana, USA) : *I Will; The Chill Turned Warm*
Alexander Clarke (Michigan, USA) : *Status Update*
Durand J. Compton (Kansas, USA) : *IT IS A FINE IRISH MORNING*
Laurie Corzett (undisclosed) : *Under Cover of Lightning*
Marian Dunn (Lancashire, England) : *Watching the War*
A.D. Fallon (Kentucky, USA) : *Futility of Desire*
James Gilmore (California, USA) : *My 30th*
Sandra Hanks (Seychelles, Indian Ocean) : *"Moon Shine Supine"*
Chi Holder (Missouri, USA) : *Enduring the Storm*
Romi Jain (California, USA) : *Her New Abode*
Diane Margaret Jardel (Northern Ireland) : *The Mirror*
Michael Lee Johnson (Illinois, USA) : *Charley Plays a Tune; Kentucky Blue* / **Just Kribbe** (California, USA) : *Telegram*
Drake Mabry (Poitiers, France) : *Four Haiku*
Trevor Maynard (Surrey, England): *Redundant C; elegant grace eternal* / **Marli Merker Moreira** (Burgos, Spain) : *Dead Woman*
Debbie Edwards Morton (Ohio, USA) : *What Will Happen?*
Gillian Prew (Argyll, Scotland) : *Birds and Bombs* / **Nancy Pritchard** (Missouri, USA) : *Moon Madness; Trouble on the Line*
Sarah Rahman (Karachi, Pakistan) : *The Worrying Whys Within*
Rainbow Reed (England) : *The Storm*
Gill C Shaw (Lancashire, England) : *Peace of Big Bear*
Michael Shepherd (Somerset, England) : *In Expectation of Rain*
Peter Alan Soron (undisclosed) : *the grand I; Tough Call in E.Z. City*
Tom Spencer (Indiana, USA) : *Festival of Souls*
N. A'Yara Stein (Indiana, USA) : *Saudade; La Nuit Blanche*
Ashleigh Stevens (London, England) : *I feel like dancing in the night*
Tom Watts (Surrey, England) : *The World's Waif*
Mark Jason Welch (Barbados): *The Truth about Oranges*

Poetry by Trevor Maynard

Grey Sun, Dark Moon (2015)
ISBN-10: 1517095255
ISBN-13: 978-1517095253

Keep on Keepin' On (2012)
ISBN-10: 1480052493
ISBN-13: 978-1480052499

Love, Death, and the War on Terror (2009)
ISBN-10: 1445206625
ISBN-13: 978-1445206622

Plays by Trevor Maynard

Four Truths (2012)
Compilation of four one-act plays
ISBN-10: 1466453397
ISBN-13: 978-1466453395

Glass (2010)
ISBN-10: 1445233231
ISBN-13: 978-1445233239

From Pillow To Post (2010)
ISBN-10: 0955851416
ISBN-13: 978-0955851414

Also published by Willowdown Books

Echoes in the Earth (2016)
by Pushpita Awasthi
(Edited by Trevor Maynard)
ISBN-10: 1480108804
ISBN-13: 978-1480108806

Professor Pushpita Awasthi is a widely published Indian
poet, Director, the Hindi Universe Foundation
Email: Info@pushpitaawasthi.com
Hindi blog: http://pushpitaawasthi.blogspot.in ; English
blog: http://poetpushpita.blogspot.in/
Further details at
http://www.thepoeticbond.com/ECHOESweb.htm

"Through the twin themes of Nature and Love,
Pushpita's work not only illuminates humanity as a
whole, but her own human relationship with the human
world. These elements of being human are interwoven
skilfully, creating a poetic expression that has depth,
articulates understanding, and possesses empathy."

Back Cover, ECHOES IN THE EARTH, © 2016

"Pushpita's work swirls with energy: darting and
surprising, leaping and resting, comforting and
challenging. Energy which, it was my role to find melody
and harmony, to bring together in such a way as the
work would flow with the ease of the Ganges, intrinsic to
the soul of humanity, of the planet, and of the universe.
This collection is therefore, a journey - a spiritual,
philosophical, and human journey."

From EDITING ECHOES by Trevor Maynard, © 2016

The Watcher from the Beacon (2010)
by Peter Alan Soron
(Edited by Trevor Maynard)

ISBN-10: 1480108804
ISBN-13: 978-1480108806

A collection of poetry from Nature, and from the edge of imagination, for the Human Condition is where Mankind thrashes against himself, defying logic, embracing logic, both spiritual and reductionist. Sometimes a poem comes from the merest tangent of thought, sometimes from a colour, sometimes from a feeling of outrage, and sometimes from the ecstasy of love. Sometimes it is fully formed, sometimes it requires further input from the reader, sometimes it tells you something, sometimes it avoids telling you anything, and sometimes you can just feel the words fall upon your body and seep into your consciousness. These poems are all the above.

*

Coming Soon from Willowdown Books

The Death of Swans (2017)
by GK Grieve
(Edited by Trevor Maynard)

ISBN-10: 1548988936
ISBN-13: 978-1548988937

The first collection by G K. Grieve is currently in process, details at www.gkgrieve.com

Willowdown Books Listing

The Poetic Bond VII
poetry anthology, edited by Trevor Maynard
planned publication November 2017
ISBN: TBC

The Death of Swans
a poetry collection by by GK Grieve
August 2017
ISBN: 978-1548988937

The Poetic Bond VI
poetry anthology, edited by Trevor Maynard,
November 2016
ISBN: 978-1539334682

Echoes in the Earth
a selection of poems by Pushpita Awasthi
November 2016
ISBN: 978-1533618801

Grey Sun, Dark Moon
a collection of poems by Trevor Maynard, 2015
ISBN: 978-1517095253

The Poetic Bond V
poetry anthology, edited by Trevor Maynard, 2015
ISBN: 978-1517783808

The Poetic Bond IV
poetry anthology, edited by Trevor Maynard, 2014
ISBN: 978-1503034525

The Poetic Bond III
poetry anthology, edited by Trevor Maynard, 2013
ISBN: 978-1492384199

Keep on Keepin' On
a poetry collection by Trevor Maynard, 2012
ISBN: 978-1480052499

The Poetic Bond II
poetry anthology, edited by Trevor Maynard, 2012
ISBN: 978-1480209732

The Poetic Bond
poetry anthology, edited by Trevor Maynard, 2011
ISBN: 978-1466498419

Four Truths
Contains four one act plays, 2011
She (1994*) From Pillow to Post (1991*), Graye (1996*), and Taciturn (1989*); (*performance dates)
ISBN, 978-1466453395

From Pillow to Post
One-act play, 2010 (performance 1991)
ISBN 978-0955851414

Glass
Full-length play, 2010 (performance 1995)
ISBN 978-1445233239

Love, Death, and the War of Terror
a poetry collection by Trevor Maynard, 2009
ISBN 978-1445206622

LOVE, LIGHT AND PEACE

74585203R00085

Made in the USA
Columbia, SC
03 August 2017